Missing

FRANCES ITANI

Missing

Grass Roots Press

First published in 2011 by Grass Roots Press

The Good Reads series is funded in part by the Government of Canada's Office of Literacy and Essential Skills.

Grass Roots Press also gratefully acknowledges the financial support for its publishing programs provided by the following agencies: the Government of Canada through the Canada Book Fund and the Government of Alberta through the Alberta Foundation for the Arts.)

Grass Roots Press would also like to thank ABC Life Literacy Canada for their support. Good Reads® is used under licence from ABC Life Literacy Canada.

Library and Archives Canada Cataloguing in Publication

Itani, Frances, 1942–
    Missing / Frances Itani.

(Good reads series)
ISBN 978–1–926583–36–5

    1. Readers for new literates. I. Title. II. Series: Good reads series (Edmonton, Alta.)

PS8567.T35M58 2011   428.6'2   C2011–903263–5

Printed and bound in Canada.

Distributed to libraries and educational and community organizations by
Grass Roots Press
www.grassrootsbooks.net

Distributed to retail outlets by
HarperCollins Canada Ltd.
www.harpercollins.ca

For the missing—men, women, and children—
and for those who are left to mourn

Chapter One

March 4, 1917
A village in northern France

Luc Caron was twelve years old when the black object fell from the sky. He had never seen anything like this before, and he didn't stop to think. He ran as fast as he could towards the place he thought the object would land.

This was a time of war, a terrible war that people would later call World War I. Already, it had lasted almost three years. More than one year ago, the Germans had captured Luc's village in northern France. Not all of France was occupied by the Germans, only a small part in the north and east. But Luc's village was one of the unlucky ones.

Fighting and shelling had destroyed many houses and roads and shops. Soldiers had moved in and taken over. Men of fighting age were taken prisoner and sent to Germany. There, they were forced to work in factories.

The old men, along with the women and children, stayed on in the village. Farmers continued to farm, and shopkeepers kept the shops open. Women did the laundry and hung it out in the wind to dry. Children went to school. Two sisters baked bread in the bakery. The blacksmith, an old man, put shoes on the horses and repaired farm tools. The priest, also an old man, visited the sick and said Mass, but that was all. The villagers had to obey the new rules. They could not leave their houses after eight o'clock at night. The only time they could meet in groups was when they went to church.

The soldiers gave orders; the villagers did as they were told. There were soldiers everywhere, checking to see that people obeyed. But no one had ever said what to do if you saw something falling from the sky. Something like the black object that twelve-year-old Luc saw on that Sunday morning in 1917.

Ten minutes earlier, just after eleven o'clock, Luc had left the village church. In the sermon, the old priest had talked about hope that the war would soon end. After three years, the village had suffered enough. The people in the parish listened with their own quiet hope. When they left the church, they hurried back to their homes to take up their hard lives again.

Luc's mother had gone home ahead of her son to prepare the noon meal. She and Luc lived alone in a small house at the far end of the village. Luc's father had been a soldier, but he had died two years ago, while fighting the Germans. Luc's mother was now a widow.

Luc was not in a hurry, and he did not go straight home with his mother after church. He pictured her in the kitchen, making his lunch, slicing a bit of pork from the bone. She would be looking out the window while she sliced, wondering where he was and why he hadn't come home. Now that his father was dead, she worried about him all the time. She watched to see if he had buttoned his jacket and wrapped his scarf around his neck. Every day, she warned him to dress warmly so he wouldn't catch a cold.

Luc liked to prowl around the village, to see if he could find out what was going on. He was always alert, always watching, ready to run if any soldiers came too close. He practised spying whenever he could, but if the soldiers saw him, they shouted and told him to go home. Still, that didn't stop him from snooping.

Luc shivered on this cold and bitter morning, but he took his time and walked slowly along a dirt path. He held a stick in his hand, and he poked it at the ground and under bushes. He was looking for small treasures. Stones that glinted of silver, old birds' nests, shiny buttons that had fallen from uniforms. One afternoon, Luc had been lucky. He had found a German coin that one of the soldiers had dropped. He kept his treasures in his bedroom, some on a small table, some on the windowsill. He hid the best ones in a canvas bag under his narrow bed.

Luc picked up a sharp pink rock and turned it over in the palm of his hand. At the same moment, he heard the sound of pecks and rattles coming from far above. He knew, right away, that he was hearing machine guns. Long ago, he had learned the pattern of sound when airplanes were fighting in the sky.

He looked up quickly and saw three airplanes. He could tell by the markings that two were German and one was British. The aerial fight was high in the sky, directly overhead. The planes dipped and dived so close to one another, Luc was certain they would crash. The two German planes circled and darted after the British plane, which made daring loops as it tried to escape. The machine guns kept shooting. The pecks and rattles went on and on while the planes buzzed through the sky.

Luc was excited by this fight in the sky. He hoped the pilot in the British plane would get away safely. He did not want the Germans to win, but with two airplanes attacking one, this was not an even fight. Although the aerial fight was terrible to watch, Luc was thrilled to see the skill of all three pilots.

Suddenly Luc was afraid. He wanted to shout out. But before he could make a sound, the British airplane flipped upside down. And that is when something large and dark fell out of the plane.

Luc ran as fast as his legs would run. When he came near the falling object, he thought his eyes were fooling him. The object looked like a large black bird gliding to earth. Only a bird could glide so slowly. But that was a crazy thought and made no sense at all. Why would a large bird fall from a plane and drift down through the sky?

The two German airplanes dipped their wings and flew off. The buzzing of their engines faded as they vanished from sight. The British plane, still upside down, dived at a sure and even angle between earth and sky. It headed away from the edge of the village and towards some trees. But Luc did not run to the trees. Instead, he ran as fast as he could to the place where he thought the black object would land.

As he came near, Luc understood his mistake. This was not a large bird at all, nothing like a bird. It was a man, a pilot, falling straight down to earth out of the sky. His thick, black coat had puffed out around him. From the ground, the ballooning coat had looked like a small, dark parachute. It must have slowed the pilot's fall a little, and that is why he seemed to be gliding.

The pilot was wearing a tight-fitting flyer's helmet. His arms were stretched out wide. He was coming in feet first, faster and faster, nearly at the ground. Now, Luc could see where the pilot would land. He would land on a pond, and the pond was covered with ice.

Chapter Two

Northern France

Luc watched in horror as the pilot slammed into the frozen pond. But the pilot did not sink through to the water below, even though the ice cracked under him. Nothing moved. Everything was still. The body lay on top of the ice. Not a drop of blood could be seen.

From the edge of the pond, Luc could now see the face of a young man. The face looked peaceful, as if the pilot were asleep. Luc knew the man had not survived. And because the body was far out on the ice, Luc also knew he could do nothing to help.

Luc was overcome by what had just happened, and he began to sob. His narrow chest heaved and he bent forward. He straightened, then bent forward again. He could not control himself, and he could not stop crying. A pilot had fallen from the sky, and no one but Luc had seen him crash down to the ice.

Luc cried even harder when he realized that he was the only witness to this person's death. He could not reach the dead pilot, because to walk on the ice would be too dangerous. So he sat on the ground and pressed his forehead to his knees, and he wondered what to do. When he heard soldiers running towards the pond, he stood up again.

After that, everything happened quickly. The soldier in charge sent two others to get iron hooks, a team of horses, and a cart. Minutes later, they returned, and they began to cast the big hooks over the pond. Finally, they snagged the pilot's body and began to drag it towards them. As they dragged, the body bumped across the unstable ice. The horses inched forward and back nervously, while they waited.

When the soldiers finally pulled the body onto shore, they lifted it and laid it on the cart. One soldier looked closely at the pilot, and Luc heard him say the word "Canadian." So this was a Canadian pilot, who had died so sadly.

Another soldier came over to Luc, who was still crying loudly at the edge of the pond. The soldier was angry, and he began to shout.

"What's the matter with you, boy? Get out of here and go home. This does not concern you. It is not your business. Go home to your mother and stay inside your house. You should not have come here."

Luc ran away from the pond, but he turned once to look back. He saw the soldiers as they walked beside the horse-drawn cart. From the direction they were headed, Luc knew exactly where they were going. The soldiers planned to take the dead pilot to the village church.

Again, Luc did not go home. Instead, he ran ahead of the Germans and hid in some bushes at the side of the church. He was careful to stay hidden when the soldiers arrived. They banged at the heavy oak doors at the front of the church and called loudly for the priest.

Luc stood up and peered through a window. He could see the old priest eating his lunch in a small office inside the building. The priest heard the banging, left his food, and went to open the main doors. The soldiers pushed their way inside and ordered the priest to clear a long table at the back of the church.

The priest cleared the table and stood back while the soldiers laid out the body. They took off the pilot's soft leather helmet and straightened his uniform and black leather coat.

After the soldiers went away, the priest said a prayer over the body. Then he went back to his office to finish his lunch. Luc had watched all of this from his hiding place outside.

Luc did not know what to do next. Because he was so late, he knew his mother would be worried. But he could not go home. Not after all that had happened. He suddenly thought of the airplane. He remembered the direction of the plane after the pilot had fallen out. It would have crashed somewhere outside the village, not near the pond at all.

Luc decided to look for the crash site. He thought carefully about the aerial fight. The plane had been headed towards some woods about a kilometre from the frozen pond. Luc knew, too, that the soldiers would also be searching. They would want to examine the plane.

Luc had lived in the village since birth, and he knew the fields and trees in every direction. He was sure he could find the plane, and he wanted to find it before the Germans did. Once more, he began to run, and he ran until he was out of breath.

He found the crash site quickly. He checked around, but saw no one. He had arrived first, which meant that the soldiers were searching some other area.

At once, Luc saw pieces of the airplane scattered everywhere. He was shocked at the way the wood and canvas had been torn apart. The wings had come off and were bent and broken. The force of the crash had driven the engine deep into the hard ground.

Because Luc knew that the Germans would soon find the place, he looked around for a souvenir. He wanted to grab something and run home with it before he was caught. He began to dig at a large piece of canvas, and he tugged and tore until two strips came loose. Clumps of dirt stuck to both. He stuffed the two pieces of canvas inside his jacket so that no one could see them.

Again, Luc looked around, and this time he saw the wooden propeller. Even in the shadows of the trees, the propeller shone with a high polish. The crash had broken it to splinters, so Luc tried to pull a small piece away from a bigger piece. After much effort, he was able to break off one splinter. He stuck this inside his jacket, hiding it beside the two canvas strips he had already taken.

Looking around one last time, Luc saw a torn card that might be a piece of map or a chart. Maybe the pilot's name was on it. Luc wanted to know this name, so he picked up the card and tried to read the printed words. But the card was damaged, and one edge had been torn off. At the same moment, Luc felt a strong hand on his shoulder—the hand of a soldier. The Germans had finally found the crash site. When Luc looked up, he recognized the soldier who had shouted at him at the pond. The soldier grabbed the piece of card away from Luc and shouted again.

"What do you think you're doing? I told you before to go home to your mother. Get away from here and don't touch anything or you will be in trouble. Go on, get away now. I never want to see you at this place again. Don't ever come back."

Luc was afraid. But the soldier did not know about Luc's hidden treasures. He did not know about the two pieces of canvas and the splinter of wood from the propeller. Pressing his arms to his chest so his treasures would not fall out of his jacket, Luc turned and ran away. This time, he ran straight home.

Chapter Three

Northern France

Luc let himself in at the back door. He tried to be quiet, but his mother heard him and called out.

"Luc, why are you so late? Where have you been? Have you been getting into trouble?"

"I was only on my way home," Luc called back. "I wasn't in any trouble."

Because his room was near the back door, Luc went there first. He took off his jacket and hid the three pieces he had taken from the crashed airplane. He stuffed his new treasures into his canvas bag. Then he pushed the bag back under his narrow bed.

Luc was so upset, he couldn't eat. He told his mother he wasn't hungry, but she paid no attention. She served him a slice of pork and a steaming potato she had baked in the fireplace. But Luc just sat there and stared at the food. He had no appetite. He could only think about all that had happened in the short space of one morning.

Luc was also hot because he had run all the way home. There were circles of red on his cheeks. He tried not to think of the threats made by the German soldier. His mother put her hand up to his forehead.

"You must have a fever," she told him. "Just look at your red face. You must be sick if you have no appetite. Why don't you lie on your bed for a while?"

Luc decided not to tell his mother what he had seen. He didn't want her to worry. He went back to his room and lay on top of his bed. He kept thinking about the pilot who had fallen out of the sky. He knew the pilot was Canadian. He had heard the German soldier say the word. A Canadian from far away across the ocean had flown a British plane that was now lying in pieces in the woods.

Luc got up quietly and put on his jacket. He slipped out the back door again because he didn't want his mother to make a fuss. And now, there was only one place he wanted to go.

Luc ran to the church and pushed open the heavy door. No one else was around. The pilot's body lay on the long table, his head turned towards the window. In the light, his face held the peaceful expression Luc had seen earlier, when the body had fallen to the ice.

In that damp and stuffy room, Luc kneeled beside the table and said a prayer. The Germans had not left a guard behind, and Luc could not bear to see the pilot's body all alone. He felt so sorry for the young man, he decided to stay until someone told him to go home. And because Luc wanted to learn the pilot's name, he decided to ask questions. He would keep snooping around. He planned to eavesdrop on the soldiers until he could find out what he needed to know.

Luc did not have long to wait in the church. A few minutes later, the old priest returned. He spoke kindly when he saw Luc.

"You are a good boy to watch over the pilot's body," he said. "This afternoon he will be put into a coffin. What a pity. His family won't even know he is dead. The war, the war." He shook his head sadly, and he, too, kneeled to say a prayer.

The next morning, almost everyone in the village came out of their houses to attend the funeral. To Luc's surprise, many German soldiers arrived just as the service was about to begin. Afterwards, the soldiers formed two lines, facing each other, in the church aisle. The coffin was carried out between the lines. Outside, a German military band played a slow funeral march.

The arrival of a German general from a nearby village was even more of a surprise. The general had come because pilots were honoured, even if they fought on the opposite side of the war. The same men who would shoot down another man's plane would line up to mourn the dead pilot. On this day, when the Canadian pilot's coffin was carried to the graveyard, German soldiers marched along behind. The people in Luc's village had never seen a ceremony like this one.

Later in the week, Luc returned alone to the graveyard. A wooden cross made from two pieces of propeller was pushed into the earth over the new grave. Luc looked at the name printed by hand on the cross. He remembered the torn card that had been lying on the ground. So that's where the soldiers had found the name.

Luc memorized the spelling: *Jack Green, R.F.C.* He knew that R.F.C. stood for Royal Flying Corps. When he returned home, he dragged his bag of treasures out from under his bed and opened it. He printed *Jack Green, R.F.C.*, on one of the canvas strips. He added the date of the pilot's death, March 4, 1917. Then he placed the piece of canvas back in the bag and shoved the bag under his bed again. Luc didn't know what he would do with the three souvenirs he had hidden. He knew only that he wanted to keep them, and that they were important.

Luc was certain that he would always remember the Canadian pilot who had died after falling from an airplane. For him, the man was a hero. And there was something else Luc would never forget. He was the only person who had witnessed the death of this brave man.

Later in the spring, Luc took white roses from his mother's garden and laid them on the pilot's grave. But this was forbidden. To the Germans, the man buried there was still their enemy. Every time the boy laid flowers on the grave, soldiers removed them and tossed them away.

Chapter Four

March 8, 1917
Nova Scotia

Four days after the plane crash in France, the sky over eastern Canada was heavy with cloud and sleet. Peggy Greenwood woke early, put on her robe, and went downstairs to light the fire. She stood beside the stove, trying to get warm, while she boiled water for her tea.

The wood box beside the stove in the kitchen was almost empty. But Peggy knew that her husband, Will, would fill it later in the morning. He stacked and stored firewood in the barn every fall, enough to last the winter.

Most days, even in winter, Will spent his time in the barn. He always had work to do on the apple farm. Tools had to be sharpened. Wood from dead trees had to be chopped. Branches pruned from trees in the orchard were cut into short lengths and tied together in bundles. These, too, were used for firewood.

Peggy heard her husband's footsteps upstairs. She had not slept well the past four nights. She had been dreaming about her son Jack, who was away in France, fighting in the war. All of her dreams were the same. Jack was flying a plane and he was in danger.

The Greenwoods had not seen Jack since he'd left home a year and a half ago. Not that they had tried to stop him. Jack had always wanted to be a pilot, and the war had given him his chance. He took flying lessons in Canada. After that, he went to England to train with the Royal Naval Air Service. Now, he was attached to the R.F.C., the Royal Flying Corps.

In January, Jack had been promoted. A framed picture of him in uniform stood on a shelf in the kitchen. He wore a leather coat, a soft leather helmet, and high boots. In the photo, he held his pilot's goggles in one hand, and he was laughing.

Peggy had Jack's most recent letter in the pocket of her robe. She had read it many times, but now she pulled it out and read it again. Jack's letters were always full of hope.

Somewhere in France

Dear Mother and Father,

I love to fly. I love to soar higher than the birds and the clouds and the trees. Farms and roads and rivers are laid out in wonderful patterns on the earth below. I wish you could see what I see from so high in the sky.

Two weeks ago I went up in a plane called a Sopwith Scout. I flew so high, I nearly froze. You must wonder why I was cold with all the clothes I have to wear. First, a layer of underwear. Then two sweaters and two layers of trousers. Over all, a fur-lined leather coat that comes almost to my knees, with a collar up to my chin. My leather helmet lined with wool and my high boots complete the picture. That cold day, I wore goggles over my eyes. On my hands, I wore fur-lined gloves.

When I landed, I had frostbite under my eyes and along the top of my nose. My goggles protected my eyes, but not the skin on my face. My friends teased me for a week and told me I looked like a raccoon.

I have been in active service for many months now, but I am safe and well. Please do not worry about me. I am trying to do my part to help end this terrible war.

Your loving son,
Jack

Jack's letters came only every few weeks. Peggy had read and folded this one so many times the paper had begun to tear. She thought about the words *active service*. She knew they meant that Jack was flying missions over German lines in the war zone.

She was not sure where Jack was located because he was not allowed to tell her. Place names were kept secret in case letters fell into enemy hands. The Germans were not supposed to know about soldiers moving from place to place or where they were going next. That is why all of Jack's letters started with the words *Somewhere in France*. Peggy understood the rule, but she still wished she knew exactly where her son was.

Peggy gave a long sigh. She wondered when the fighting would end. The war had started three years ago, in 1914. At that time, everyone believed it would be over before Christmas. But millions of men from many countries were still fighting.

Will came downstairs and sat at the table. Peggy poured his tea, and then she poured a second cup for herself. The kitchen warmed up while they ate their breakfast. There wasn't much to say when they were both thinking about their only son. Peggy wondered if she should tell Will about the dreams she'd been having. She decided not to. He, too, might have had bad dreams about Jack.

The wind suddenly rattled a window that looked out over the back garden. Past the garden, Peggy and Will could see rows of apple trees, the branches reaching to the sky. The trees were thin and bare on this cold morning, and snow covered the ground between the rows. Will reached across the table for Peggy's hand.

"You've been dreaming about Jack again, haven't you," he said. "I can tell."

She nodded, but she didn't want to talk about the dreams. She tried to smile, and he tried to smile back. Peggy saw the lines in his face. Will had aged since Jack had left for the war. Peggy knew that she, too, had aged. She kept telling herself not to worry, that a letter would come soon.

The wind stopped rattling the window at that moment, and the brass ringer twisted in the front door. The noise made Will stand up too quickly. He almost lost his balance as he walked towards the front of the house. He and Peggy both knew the mail did not arrive this early. They had always feared that someone would come to the door and hand them a cablegram with a message they did not want.

The messenger on the doorstep did hand Will a cablegram, sent from the War Office in England. Will carried the piece of paper to the kitchen and laid it on the table. Peggy put down her cup, but her hand shook so badly she spilled a puddle of tea over the table. She stood, and she waited. Will read the message out loud.

WE REGRET FLIGHT LIEUTENANT JACK GREENWOOD REPORTED MISSING MARCH 4. ANY FURTHER NEWS WILL BE SENT IMMEDIATELY.

Missing. Peggy and Will tried to understand the word *missing*. They stared across the puddle of cold tea, and then they moved towards each other.

"But not dead," said Peggy.

What did she say? Peggy's voice sounded far away. Will looked at the cablegram again.

Jack was missing. But missing did not mean dead. Surely not. The cablegram did not say that Jack was dead.

Did this mean that there was still hope?

A few weeks later, a letter arrived. The letter had been written by Jack's Commanding Officer, a man named Frank Bolton. Like Jack's letters, it came from *Somewhere in France*.

Dear Mr. and Mrs. Greenwood,

On March 4, 1917, your son Jack was involved in heavy fighting. While he was flying, he and two other pilots were attacked by German planes. They had a hard fight, but Jack shot down two enemy planes. After that, he became separated from the others. He might have been in another aerial fight. No one saw what happened to him. No one knows where his plane went down or if he landed safely. He has been declared missing.

If Jack had to land behind enemy lines, he might now be a prisoner. We hope that after this war is over, we will see him again. If we hear any news from the other side of the line, we will let you know right away. We miss Jack and his bright, happy ways. He never left his friends in trouble, and he was always one of the first to volunteer for duty.

All of Jack's personal things have been collected and sent to England. These items will be sent on by mail to your home in Canada. In the meantime, the other pilots and Jack's many friends here join me in saying how sorry we are. We miss our true friend.

Sincerely,
Frank Bolton

This letter gave hope to the Greenwoods. Maybe their son was a prisoner. Maybe he was alive, after all.

Peggy looked over at Jack's photo on the shelf. He was a handsome young man with dark hair and dark eyes. He was twenty-three years old and taller than his father. He was laughing, and ready for adventure.

Chapter Five

June, 1917
Somewhere in France

Three months had passed since Jack Greenwood had gone missing. On this sunny day, two pilots stood chatting outside at their base camp. One was Frank Bolton, Jack's Commanding Officer. The other was one of Jack's friends. The two men heard the buzzing of an airplane, and they looked up. A single plane flew above them, a German plane.

The enemy pilot dropped a package from the plane and quickly flew back towards the German lines. Frank Bolton and the other

R.F.C. pilot ran to see what was inside the package that had landed with a thump nearby. Frank tore it open. Inside, he found a message written on a sheet of paper.

JACK GREEN CRASHED OVER MY LINE, MARCH 4, 1917. <u>TOT</u>

Packages like this had been dropped at other times by enemy planes. The pilots on both sides of the war had a special code of honour. Sometimes, when a British or Canadian pilot died behind enemy lines, a German pilot would drop a package giving the news. The Royal Flying Corps did the same. Both sides received information about missing pilots in this way. The code of honour also helped the families of the pilots. Otherwise, years might pass before parents or wives knew if a loved one was alive or dead.

Jack Green crashed over my line, March 4, 1917. Tot. Frank Bolton knew that the German word *tot* meant "dead." No pilot named Jack Green had ever worked for him. But Frank knew that Jack Greenwood had gone missing on March 4, 1917. And, of course, the names were almost the same.

The news had to be about the same man. The Germans might have made a mistake and left off the last part of the name.

Frank handed the message to the other pilot.

"The name is *Green*, not *Greenwood*," he said. "But this must be about Jack Greenwood. What do you think?"

"I agree," said the other pilot. "The Germans wouldn't lie about a pilot's death. But this is bad news about Jack."

Frank looked through the package to see if it contained anything else. He wanted to know more of the story, because there was always more to know. Someone might have seen Jack's plane go down. Someone might know other facts. But who was that person? And where was Jack's body? Had he been buried by the Germans? Did he have a grave?

Frank was both sad and angry. Many of his pilots had been killed, and now one more was dead. Here was the proof, on a piece of paper in his hand. The proof came from the enemy and had to be believed.

The message about Jack's death could not be treated as official news. Even so, Frank knew he would have to write another letter to Jack's parents. He hated this part of his job, but the truth had to be told. Jack's mother and father in Canada were waiting for news. And their son had been so young, only twenty-three years old.

Somewhere in France

Dear Mr. and Mrs. Greenwood,

Three months have passed since I first wrote to you. I must now tell you that I have received news about Jack. I have learned that his plane crashed behind enemy lines on March 4. It is my sad duty to let you know that Jack was killed at the time of the crash. We had hoped that his plane had landed safely and that he was a prisoner, but that did not happen.

I am so sorry to send such bad news. But Jack died the death of a hero. He served his King and country well. Every one of us is proud to have known such a fine man. You should be proud of him, too.

If you want to write to me, I will be glad to hear from you. I wish I knew more about the details of Jack's death. If I learn anything else, I will write to you immediately.

Sincerely,
Frank Bolton

This was not the only letter received by the Greenwoods. Two official letters were also sent, both from England. The first was from the War Office.

London, England
June 10, 1917

Dear Mr. and Mrs. Greenwood,

I must inform you that word about your son, Flight Lieutenant Jack Greenwood, has been received from a German source. He was killed March 4, 1917, when his plane was brought down in the German lines.

We send our deep regrets.

The second letter, sent on behalf of the King and Queen, came from an office in Buckingham Palace. Their Majesties, said the letter, had learned with deep regret that the death of Jack Greenwood had now been confirmed. The King and Queen were very, very sorry.

Chapter Six

Summer, 1917
Nova Scotia

The Greenwoods read the three letters about Jack's death many times. Now they knew there was nothing left to hope for. Frank Bolton, Jack's Commanding Officer, had even said in his letter that they should be proud. But why should they be proud? How could they be proud when the son they lost was so dear to them?

Peggy and Will could not bear to talk to each other about their son's death. Not until much later. The thought of Jack's plane crashing to earth caused them too much pain. During the day, they tried to carry on. In the night, each of them heard the other crying.

Every morning, Will went out to the barn to begin the day's work. Taking care of the orchard kept him busy from sunrise to sunset. He was glad to have something to do. The hard work helped him to stop thinking about Jack's death.

Indoors, Peggy kept the blinds closed. Most of the time, the house was dark and in shadow. She walked through the rooms and asked herself the same questions, over and over. *Where did Jack's plane go down? Where did it crash? Where is our son buried? His body has to be in a grave somewhere. But where?*

If only she could learn the answers to these questions. But the war continued, and she had no way of finding out.

One day, when Will was outside in the orchard, Peggy went upstairs to Jack's bedroom. She opened the dresser drawer and looked at the pile of letters Jack had sent home. Beside them lay his belongings, which had been sent from England after his plane had gone missing.

Peggy lifted the items out of the drawer and set them on the bed. Jack's shaving kit. His identity card. His log book.

The log book was so small, it could fit in the palm of Peggy's hand. She opened it slowly and turned the pages, knowing that Jack had held the same book in his own two hands. He had started the log while training in England. Every time he had flown an airplane, he'd recorded times and distances and the type of plane. He'd added detailed notes about fog and wind and weather.

Jack had written about his first solo flight on page 4 of the log. That must have been a special day for him. At the bottom of each page, he had added up all the minutes and hours he spent flying through the skies. One of his instructors had written a special note after Jack had flown sixty hours. The note said that Jack was ready for *active service*, ready to carry out patrols and missions.

After that, Jack made an entry in the log about the day he started "bomb dropping." Peggy did not like to read about "bomb dropping." When Jack's plane had crashed, he had flown a total of one hundred hours.

Peggy closed the small book, walked over to the window, and opened the blind. She looked up to a blue sky, and she felt the sun warm her through the glass. She opened the window to let in some fresh air, went back to the bed, and sat down. She thought about the kind of child Jack had been when he was a small boy. He had always wanted to be a pilot.

When Jack was four years old, he began to fold and cut paper into the shapes of airplanes. He stood on a chair and sailed his paper planes through the kitchen. He laughed and sang and made up stories about flying.

As he grew older, he built toy airplanes out of wood and strips of cloth. He began to read books and magazines about "flying machines." Many of these stories were about men and women who tested the new machines in the air.

Peggy thought about all of these things, and more. She thought about how safe and happy the family had been when Jack was living at home. Then, in 1914, war broke out. Young men from all parts of Canada became soldiers and left home. Nurses and doctors, too. All had sailed across the Atlantic Ocean from Halifax to England. After that, they were sent to France or to other battlefields. Many of these young people had been killed. Like Peggy, millions of mothers were grieving.

Peggy returned to the dresser and lifted Jack's letters from the drawer. She put them on the bed beside his belongings. She and Will had read every letter many times. She pulled one out of the pile and read it again. Jack had sent this letter from England during his first year away from home.

Dear Mother and Father,

The training is not easy but I don't mind hard work. You know how I love to learn new things. The men I am training with are good fellows, and I have many new friends.

The apples you sent arrived in a parcel in the mail, along with the chocolate bars and gloves and stockings. Thank you for wrapping each apple in paper. Not one went bad. I was even able to share them with my friends. What a treat to get a great parcel like this from home!

I have to tell you that the apples reminded me of the orchard, and of the rows of healthy trees. I thought of the sun on the blossoms in spring. I thought of the clear air in the fall, and I wished I could be there to help. Father, I hope you were able to hire someone to help with the picking. So many apples, so many trees. How could I ever forget?

Thank you also for knitting stockings for me, Mother. They are a perfect fit and help to keep my feet warm and dry.

Please do not worry about me. I am doing what I want to do. I am careful and I am safe.

Your loving son,
Jack

When Peggy closed her eyes, she thought of planes soaring and darting and looping through the clouds. She tried not to think of Jack falling down, down, down. How she hated the war. If only the fighting and the killing would stop. Then, maybe, she would finally be able to find out where Jack was buried. His body had to be somewhere.

But Peggy also knew that she would never board a ship in Halifax to sail across the Atlantic Ocean. She would never see Jack's grave. Her son might not even have a grave, and that was the worst thing of all. Not knowing if Jack's body had been buried.

Peggy decided to ask Will to write to the War Office to find out if there was any more news. If only they could find out even one detail about Jack's death. But this would probably never happen. Even so, the war had to be over soon. It had to be.

Chapter Seven

Nova Scotia

World War I ended in November 1918. The fighting stopped at eleven o'clock in the morning on the eleventh day of the eleventh month. After four years, more than nine million soldiers had died in different parts of the world. Millions more were wounded or missing. No one could have imagined such suffering or such huge losses.

After the war, Jack's photo stayed on the shelf in the Greenwood kitchen at the apple farm. Medals were now displayed beside the photo. When friends and family came to visit, they all wanted to see the photo and the medals. Everyone said Jack was a hero, but that did not make his parents feel any better.

Will Greenwood continued to write letters to the War Office. He sent letters again and again, always hoping for news. He wanted to know if Jack's grave had been found. The reply was always the same. Nothing new was known.

Will truly wondered if Jack's grave would ever be found. He kept reading about the missing, the millions of soldiers from so many countries who had no graves. He did not even know the name of the place in France where Jack's plane had crashed. Was it a town? A village? Someone must know. Will decided that he would never give up.

Will learned that a special War Graves office had opened in England, with its head office in London. Later, another office opened in Ottawa because so many Canadian soldiers had no known graves. The Greenwoods weren't the only ones trying to find out where a beloved son was buried.

Because Will kept writing letters, he received letters in reply. Twice a year, he wrote to the War Graves office. Twice a year, a man named Mr. Harvey replied.

London, England

Dear Sir,

I have all of your letters here on my desk. The name of your son, Jack Greenwood, is well known to this office. We have tried to locate his grave, but, so far, we have not done so. Finding it will take time, because so many millions of men went missing.

After the war, the Germans gave us their burial lists. If we can match Jack's name to a name on any of the lists, we will write to you immediately. I am sorry that I have no further news to give you at this time.

Sincerely,

T. S. Harvey
Assistant Secretary

Will was disappointed each time a new letter came from the War Graves office, but he never gave up hope. Maybe Jack's name would be on one of the German burial lists. Will promised Peggy that he would never stop sending letters. Not until Jack's grave had been found.

Every year on Jack's birthday, the first of July, Peggy and Will went upstairs to Jack's bedroom. They opened the drawer of their son's dresser and took out his personal belongings. These were all they had from Jack's time away at the war. The shaving kit. The identity card. The log book. The pile of letters.

The Greenwoods set everything on top of Jack's bed. They opened the log book, read a few of the letters, and talked about Jack when he had been a small boy. This yearly ritual helped them to remember what a happy child Jack had been, and it helped them with their grief. They returned Jack's belongings to the drawer, and they did not open it again until the first of July the following year.

Chapter Eight

1928
Northern France

But what about Luc Caron, the boy living in the small village in northern France? The boy who had been twelve years old when the pilot fell from the sky on March 4, 1917.

Luc was now twenty-three years old. Ten years had passed since the war had ended. The Germans had lost the war, and the soldiers in the village had returned to Germany. The villagers slowly repaired and rebuilt their roads, houses, and shops. Luc was now married, and he and his wife lived in their own small house in the village. They had a one-year-old baby boy.

From the time Luc had finished school, he had worked on a farm owned by his uncle. The farm was outside the village, not far from where the airplane had crashed. Every morning, Luc got up early and rode his bicycle from his home to the farm. During the winter months, he walked. Few people owned cars, but every family had a bicycle.

Luc worked hard on his uncle's farm. He loved to be outside, and he loved to drive the team of horses. He loved the smells in the air at haying time, and he enjoyed taking care of the animals. He was suited to farming, and he wanted to stay on the land. To support himself and his family, he was saving money to buy a small farm of his own.

His mother needed his help, too. Mrs. Caron still lived in the small house where Luc had grown up. She kept a few hens and sold eggs. Because she was skilled with a needle and thread, she also sewed to earn extra money. Many people in the village brought cloth to her so she could make them new clothes. She had sewed Luc's wedding suit, and she was always making clothes for the baby, her only grandchild.

Luc had never forgotten his hero, the Canadian pilot buried in the graveyard next to the church. Every Sunday after Mass, Luc visited the grave. Every summer for eleven years, he had placed roses below the cross made from the two pieces of propeller.

Luc had told the story of the pilot's death to his wife and friends. But he was always sorry that he couldn't share the story with the family of the dead pilot. If only he could meet them. He wanted to tell them about the day Jack Green fell from his plane and crashed to the ice on the pond. Luc felt as if he had become part of the pilot's story.

The souvenirs Luc had taken from the site of the plane crash were still important to him. Ever since that day, he had kept the strips of canvas and the splinter of wood from the propeller. When the war ended and the Germans left, Luc no longer had to hide anything. He took the items out of the canvas bag and wrapped them in a piece of cloth. Now he kept the bundle on a shelf in his home.

Once a year, on March 4, Luc pulled the bundle off the shelf and opened it. Clumps of dirt still stuck to the strips of canvas, just as they had on the day of the crash. Luc could still read the name and date he had printed on one of the strips. The three items were very dear to Luc. They were part of the dead pilot's story, but they were part of Luc's story, too.

One Sunday after Mass, Luc noticed a black car parked on the road outside the church. He knew immediately that it was the car of a stranger.

Luc went around the side of the church to the graveyard. The sun was shining on this beautiful Sunday in May. Trees were in blossom, and flowers lay on some of the graves. He walked towards the grave he knew so well. The name *Jack Green, R.F.C.* was still printed on the roughly made cross. The words on the cross were still clear.

But on this day, a man, a stranger, was standing beside the grave. The man stared down at the cross and checked a piece of paper in his hand. He pulled a pen from his pocket and wrote something on the paper. When Luc came closer, he saw that the paper in the man's hand was some kind of list.

"Are you someone from this man's family?" Luc asked the stranger. "Did you know Jack Green? He was a Canadian pilot who died March 4, 1917."

The man looked up, surprised to see Luc. He was even more surprised that Luc knew the date of the pilot's death. The two men shook hands.

"I'm from the War Graves office in England," said the man. "I'm looking for the grave of a pilot named Jack Greenwood. But the name on this grave is Jack Green."

"That is the name the Germans printed on the cross in 1917," said Luc. "I was a boy at the time, and I remember every detail. I attended the pilot's funeral. Jack Green is the only pilot buried in this graveyard. The other graves belong to village people."

"How do you know the pilot was Canadian?" asked the man.

"I heard the German soldiers say the word *Canadian*," said Luc. "The soldiers must have been able to tell, but I don't know how."

"Are you sure about the date?" asked the man.

"I'm absolutely sure," said Luc. "I will never forget March 4, 1917. I saw the plane flip upside down, and I watched the pilot fall to the ground. I was very much upset, especially because I was the only person who saw him fall to his death. Three planes were fighting in the sky that Sunday morning, and I happened to be walking directly below. I was only a boy, and I was trying to spy on the Germans who had invaded our village. The other people who live here were inside their houses and didn't see what happened. Jack Green, who is buried here, was flying a British plane. He tried to fight two German planes at the same time. The fight was over quickly."

"The Germans gave us their burial lists at the end of the war," said the stranger. "That is why I'm here. The War Graves office in England saw from the lists that one soldier was buried in this village. But no one knew the soldier was a pilot. If you look at the German list I have here, you'll see the name, *Jack Green*. But neither the list nor the cross has any date. If you are certain about the date, then this has to be the grave I'm looking for. Jack Greenwood was a Canadian pilot who went missing on that very day, March 4, 1917."

"Maybe the Germans copied Jack Green's name from the torn card," said Luc.

"What torn card?"

"A torn card was lying on the ground near the pieces of the airplane," said Luc. "I was at the crash site before the soldiers got there, but when they saw me they chased me away. I had already hidden three things inside my jacket. When I picked up the piece of card, I saw a name, but the edge of the card was torn. I tried to keep that, too, but a German soldier grabbed it out of my hand."

"So part of the name was torn off in the crash," said the man. "That might be why the grave was not identified sooner. The names *Jack Green* and *Jack Greenwood* are almost the same, it's true. But millions of soldiers have no graves, and our lists are very long. There were many soldiers named Green and many named Greenwood."

"You are the first person to come here to identify the grave," said Luc. "I am sure of that."

"The date you have given me, March 4, 1917, is the exact date Jack Greenwood went missing," said the man.

"If it's a pilot you are looking for, then this has to be the same man," said Luc.

"I'd like to hear the whole story before our office confirms the identity," said the man. "I would like to send word to the Greenwood family in Canada. They have been waiting many years for news. They will be glad to know if we have finally found their son's grave."

"Please come to my home," said Luc. "I, too, have waited many years. And now I would like to tell my story."

Chapter Nine

1928
Northern France

Luc brought the stranger to his home. As they walked, he thought about what he would say. He wanted to tell the man about the peaceful look on the pilot's face after he'd crashed to the ice on the pond. About how he had cried when he knew he could do nothing to help. About how he had kept the details of that day in his memory.

He also wanted to tell the man about the German soldiers. How they brought a team of horses and a cart to the pond. How they used hooks to pull the body to shore. How they loaded the pilot's body onto the cart and took it to the church. And Luc wanted to tell about hiding in the bushes under the church window. About watching the priest clear the long table where the body would lie. And about the funeral, too. How a German military band played music, and how a German general attended. And how the villagers had never seen such an event before.

Most of all, Luc wanted to show the man what was in the bundle on the shelf. The bundle he had kept for eleven years.

Luc invited the man to sit at the table in the kitchen. The room smelled of newly baked bread. Luc's wife had been up since early morning. She welcomed the stranger and served tea and slices of fresh bread with butter and jam. The baby was asleep in a special cradle in a corner near the kitchen fireplace.

"What did you hide in your jacket?" the man asked, after he'd had his tea. "I'd really like to see what you found at the crash site."

"I'm happy to show you," said Luc. "I've kept my souvenirs ever since the day of the crash. The soldiers had no idea that I had taken anything. When they shouted at me to get away from the crash site, I ran home. I put my treasures into a canvas bag, and I hid the bag under my bed. Of course, I wasn't supposed to do that, and I was afraid. So I kept them hidden until the end of the war. But because I saw the pilot fall to his death, I felt connected to him. I wanted to have something to show his family. All these years, I have wanted to tell them what a brave death this man had."

"Maybe we should start at the beginning," said the man from the War Graves office. He took out his pen, opened his notebook, and began to write while Luc told the story.

Luc tried to remember every detail. Then he went to the shelf, carried the bundle to the kitchen table, and unwrapped the cloth. There lay the two canvas strips. There lay the splinter of wood from the propeller.

The stranger was surprised to see what Luc had kept all these years. He turned the items over in his hands. He rubbed the dirt on the canvas strips between his fingers. He studied the name and the date Luc had printed on one of the strips. Finally, he handed everything back to Luc.

"This is what I have been searching for," said the man. "What you printed on the canvas is only half the name, but the man you saw was Jack Greenwood. He was the only Canadian pilot who went missing that day. The mystery of his grave has now been solved. I have to thank you for inviting me here and telling your story."

"You said that you would write to the pilot's family in Canada," Luc said. "But after you let them know about the grave, I would like to write to them, too. Will you send me their address?"

"I'll be more than happy to do that," said the man. "You'll receive it in about two weeks. Do you want our office to send the objects from the plane crash to the family? I can take them with me today and have them sent from England."

Luc thought about this for a moment. "Yes," he said. "It's time for me to part with the souvenirs that have meant so much to me. These belong to the family of the pilot. In a few weeks, I will write to them myself. I'll tell them the story of what happened during the last moments of their son's life."

Chapter Ten

1928
Nova Scotia

One Monday morning in June, Peggy and Will Greenwood sat in the kitchen looking out at the rows of apple trees. Peggy had walked through the orchard early that morning. She'd come back into the house and baked bread, and now she made a pot of tea. Will was taking a break from his outdoor work. The brass ringer suddenly twisted in the front door, making its usual loud noise.

Will answered the door. There stood the postman, who handed over a parcel with a letter attached. Will brought these into the kitchen.

"Here we go again," he said. "Another letter from the War Graves office. But look, Peggy, they've sent a parcel this time. They've never done that before. Which one shall we open first?"

Peggy reached for the letter. "We might as well start with this one," she said.

They sat at the table and Peggy read aloud.

London, England

Dear Mr. and Mrs. Greenwood,

I am finally able to send news. We have found a war grave with the name *Jack Green* printed by hand on a cross over it. This cross had been made from two pieces of propeller from your son's plane. The graveyard is beside a church in a small village in northern France. I have written its name and location at the end of this letter.

An officer from our War Graves office travelled to France to visit the village grave site. He found proof that your son, Jack

Greenwood, is buried there. We did not know this sooner because only half of your son's name is on the cross. German soldiers had copied the name from a torn card they found at the crash site in 1917. We are certain that this "Jack Green" is your son.

We are sorry we have taken so many years to identify your son's grave. But there is more to tell. While our officer was in the village in France, he happened to meet a young man named Luc Caron. He soon learned that Mr. Caron was the only witness to the aerial fight in which your son was killed.

Mr. Caron was much affected by the tragedy that took your son's life. He was only a boy at the time, but he attended the church service and the burial of your son. He also saved three souvenirs from the crash site. These souvenirs have been sent to you from this office, and you will receive them along with this letter.

Mr. Caron asked if he might write to you directly. He wants so much to share the details of the event he witnessed so long ago.

We have given him your address. You can expect his personal letter in a few weeks.

Sincerely,

T. S. Harvey
Secretary

Jack's parents opened the parcel. They cried when they saw the strips of canvas and the splinter from the propeller. They cried, but they were glad to have real proof of what had happened to their son.

Will went to the bookshelf and carried the atlas to the table. He opened it to a map of northern France, and he and Peggy found the name of the village on the map. Now they knew that their beloved son had a grave. Now they knew the name of the place where his body was lying.

Two weeks later, the first letter from Luc Caron arrived. In the years to follow, there would be many more letters. But the first was the one Will and Peggy had been waiting for.

It told them what they wanted and needed to know: the story of their son's last moments of life.

This is how that first letter from Luc Caron began.

Dear Mr. and Mrs. Greenwood,

With deep feeling, I write this letter, having found you at last. By now you will have received the souvenirs I guarded for many years on behalf of your son. You have seen that clumps of dirt are still stuck to the canvas from the wings of your son's plane. The strips of canvas are exactly as I found them when I tore them from the ground. The splinter of propeller, I hid inside my jacket.

I part with these souvenirs sadly, because they have been so dear to me. But of course they are more dear to you, and it is to you that they now belong.

I am also sorry to open in your hearts, again, the sorrow of losing your son. I have been told by the War Graves office in England that you will want to hear my story. And so, with respect, I now start at the beginning.

In 1917, I was a small boy, only twelve years old. On March 4, a Sunday, I was on my way home from church. Just after eleven o'clock in the morning, I heard machine-gun fire in the sky above me. Two German planes were fighting a British plane. I looked up to watch this fight in the sky...

Acknowledgements

I thank C. W. Hunt and Norm Christie for responding to my questions about World War I pilots. I thank the Archives of the Canadian War Museum for permission to fictionalize a real event that happened during 1917. I first came upon the file (#19720147) while gathering information for a story I was writing. For *Missing*, I decided to expand the story into a novel based on the bare facts of the actual incident: a plane crash in France witnessed by a young boy, and the mistaken identity of a lost Canadian pilot. Because this is a work of fiction, the locations and the names and details of characters in the story are totally invented.

Good Reads

Discover Canada's Bestselling Authors with Good Reads Books

Good Reads authors have a special talent—
the ability to tell a great story, using clear language.

Good Reads books are ideal for people

＊ on the go, who want a short read;
＊ who want to experience the joy of reading;
＊ who want to get into the reading habit.

To find out more, please visit
www.GoodReadsBooks.com

The Good Reads project is sponsored by
ABC Life Literacy Canada.

The project is funded in part by the Government of Canada's
Office of Literacy and Essential Skills.

Libraries and literacy and education markets
order from Grass Roots Press.

Bookstores and other retail outlets order from HarperCollins Canada.

Good Reads Series

If you enjoyed this Good Reads book,
you can find more at your local library or bookstore.

✳

The Stalker by Gail Anderson-Dargatz

In From the Cold by Deborah Ellis

New Year's Eve by Marina Endicott

Home Invasion by Joy Fielding

The Day the Rebels Came to Town by Robert Hough

Picture This by Anthony Hyde

Shipwreck by Maureen Jennings

The Picture of Nobody by Rabindranath Maharaj

The Hangman by Louise Penny

Easy Money by Gail Vaz-Oxlade

✳

For more information on Good Reads,
visit **www.GoodReadsBooks.com**

New Year's Eve
By Marina Endicott

On New Year's Eve, Dixie and her husband Grady set off on a car trip. They plan to visit Grady's family, five hours away. But soon they're caught in a blizzard. They turn off the highway and go to their friend Ron's house. Both Grady and Ron are RCMP officers. When Ron must go out on duty, Grady goes with him.

Dixie spends the evening sharing secrets with a couple of other RCMP wives. By midnight, Dixie has learned a thing or two about marriage, and about love.

New Year's Eve leads to a turning point for Dixie and Grady. And a new road for them both.

The Day the Rebels Came to Town

By Robert Hough

The year is 1920, and all of Mexico is at war with itself. Gangs of rebels roam the country, stealing money, food, and horses. Carlos is twenty-eight years old. He works in his father's café. One day, a gang rides into Carlos's village. When the gang leaves, they kidnap Carlos.

Weeks later, the rebels and Carlos ride into the town of Rosita. Suddenly, Carlos is forced to make a life or death decision. He does so, though in a way that surprises everyone.

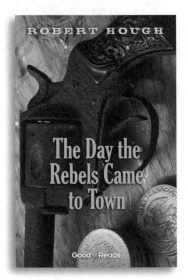

Is Carlos a brave man or a coward? It is a question that takes him a lifetime to answer.

Picture This
By Anthony Hyde

Paul Stone is an artist. One day, a beautiful woman named Zena walks into his studio. For Paul, it is love at first sight. Zena offers Paul a simple, but strange, job. When Paul takes the job, he steps into a world of trouble.

Zena is mixed up with a crook. They are planning to steal three paintings. Paul finds himself dragged into an art theft worth $3 million. As time goes on, Paul learns he is being lied to, even by Zena. Will Paul stick to the plan? Who will end up with the money? And who will go to jail?

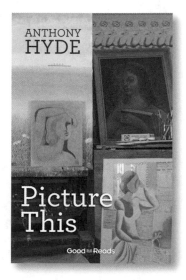

About the Author

OTTAWA PUBLIC LIBRARY FOUNDATION

Frances Itani is the author of fourteen books. Her bestselling, award-winning novel *Deafening* was translated into sixteen languages.

Frances taught and practised nursing for eight years. She began to write while studying at university and while raising a young family. She has worked as a volunteer all her life. Frances lives in Ottawa.

Also by Frances Itani:

FICTION:
Truth or Lies
Pack Ice
Man Without Face
Leaning, Leaning Over Water
Deafening
Poached Egg on Toast
Remembering the Bones
Requiem

POETRY:
No Other Lodgings
Rentee Bay
A Season of Mourning

CHILDREN'S BOOKS:
Linger By the Sea
Best Friend Trouble
(forthcoming)

*